For Pia and Isabel

Library of Congress Cataloging-in-Publication Data

Potter, Giselle, author, illustrator.

This is my dollhouse / Giselle Potter. —First edition.

pages cm

Summary: A little girl who has made her own dollhouse from a box and her vivid imagination has trouble playing with her friend Sophie's perfect dolls and dollhouse, but when Sophie comes to visit she is afraid that her handiwork will not be good enough for Sophie.

ISBN 978-0-553-52153-5 (hc : alk. paper) — ISBN 978-0-553-52154-2 (glb : alk. paper) — ISBN 978-0-553-52155-9 (ebk)

[1. Dollhouses—Fiction. 2. Imagination—Fiction.] I. Title.

PZ7.P8519Thi 2016

[E]—dc23

2015005879

The text of this book is set in Berthold Baskerville Book.

The illustrations in this book were rendered in watercolor and ink.

Book design by Rachael Cole

MANUFACTURED IN CHINA

2 4 6 8 10 9 7 5 3 1

First Edition

This Is My Dollhouse

Giselle Potter

schwartz & wade books • new york

This is my dollhouse.

It used to be just a cardboard box. But then I painted bricks on the outside and divided the inside into rooms and made wallpaper with my markers and it became almost like a real little house.

Here's my family:

Grandma Mousey

Mommy

Daddy

the twins, Lucy and Lola

I have some furniture people gave me, but mostly I make things.

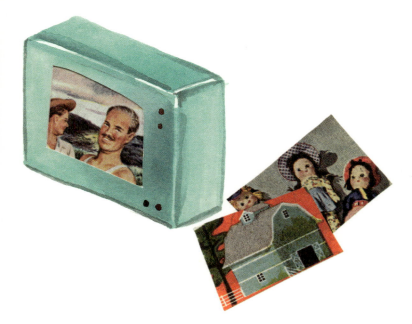

I made a TV by cutting a hole in a little silver box and gluing a picture inside. I can change the picture whenever I want.

The rug is a very small piece of carpet I cut off the one in my room. (So far, no one has noticed.)

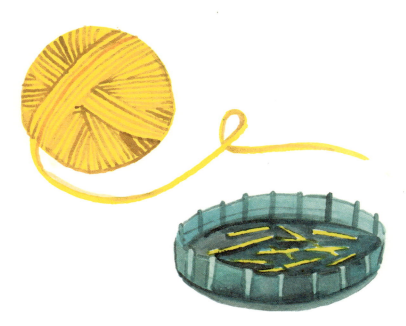

I made a stove by drawing burners on one of my blocks.

This is a plate of noodles.

Most days at the dollhouse go like this:

In the morning, Lucy and Lola get dressed up in their fancy clothes.

Mommy makes them fried eggs,

and then the twins take the elevator up, up, up and
swim in the rooftop pool in their bikinis.

Then they go down, down, down to the living
room and watch TV.
 And Daddy makes them a tiny bowl of teeny-tiny
popcorn for a snack.

YUM! they
say as they gobble it
all up.

Then they all get into their pajamas and go to sleep in one big bed

so they don't have scary dreams.

I tuck them in tight and sing them a good-night song.

My friend Sophie has a dollhouse too, but hers is all perfect.

She has a mom, a dad, and two kids she just calls "the kids."

They all look the same, with painted-on clothes and plastic hair.

Everything matches.

There is a toilet with a
lid that goes up and down.

There is a plastic refrigerator with a door that
opens. It has plastic food inside.

You don't have to make fried eggs because there
are plates with eggs painted on them.

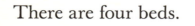

There are four beds.

And there is a matching shiny red couch and chair in the living room and a TV that always has the same picture on it.

When I come over, Sophie makes her mom hop around the kitchen and call "Breakfast!" really loud.

I make the kids hop around and sit at the yellow table in their yellow chairs.

They stare straight ahead.

Now Sophie and I don't know what to do next.

"I think they need an elevator," I say as I reach for a Dixie cup.

"That is NOT an elevator!" Sophie says. She puts the kids in front of their miniature TV on their shiny red couch.

"Let's make the family go on vacation!" I suggest.

"I don't have an airplane for them, so they can't," Sophie says firmly.

I keep quiet in case she thinks my idea for an airplane is stupid.

"How about they get a new dog and need to walk it?"

I try to fit one of Sophie's hair ties over her stuffed puppy's head.

"That is not *their* puppy!" she says.

"Okay, how about the boy kid breaks his leg and we need to bring him to the hospital to fix it?" I search her desk for some tape we can use to make a cast.

Sophie just looks at me.

It feels stuffy in her room, so we decide to go play on her swing set instead.

I worry the whole way home that I can never invite Sophie over.

She would hate my dollhouse.

But Sophie does come over.

I show her everything but my dollhouse.

"What should we play?" she asks.

I stand in front of a pile of blankets and don't say a word.

She peeks under.

"Oh!" she cries. "What about this?"
I itch my knees and swallow the
lumps in my throat.

Then somehow the cardboard box turns into my dollhouse again.

I remember my family is sleeping.

I can hear them snoring, especially Grandma Mousey.

"Time to get up!" I say, and begin to dress them.

"Can I help?" Sophie asks.

I let her.

I introduce her to Lucy and Lola, Mommy, Daddy, and Grandma Mousey.

"They are going on a tropical vacation today," I say.

We pack their suitcase with their best clothes,
their favorite snacks, and a tiny map.

Then the family gets in their private plane and it takes them far, far away.

They explore the jungle and
find a wounded tiger.

Sophie makes the mommy say,

I think his leg
is broken!

He needs to be
bandaged up!

I make the twins say.

I run to find tape and we wrap it around the tiger's leg.

"How about the family decides to take him home and keep him as their pet?" I say.

"Yeah, and they name him Stripey," Sophie says.

Then we help the doll family get into their private plane and fly home together.

We ride them up to their bedroom in the elevator cup.

We tuck the whole family and Stripey into their big cozy bed.

"Nighty-night," Sophie says, and I sing the good-night song.

"Sooophieeee, it's time to go!" we hear Sophie's mom calling.

"But I just got here!" Sophie shouts back.

"Next time we can have a birthday party for Lucy and Lola and make them cupcakes," I say.

"Maybe tomorrow?" Sophie says with big, hopeful eyes.

"Definitely tomorrow," I say . . .

and look proudly at my dollhouse.